For Tina and Anne.
I just wrote this down;
you had the courage and creativity to live it.

And for Kiva – a mother's love never, ever goes away.

Stormbird Press is an imprint of Wild Migration Limited.
PO Box 73, Parndana, South Australia.
www.stormbirdpress.com
Copyright © Alice Teasdale and Júlia Both, 2022

Apart from any use permitted under the Australian Copyright Act 1968 and subsequent amendments, no part may be reproduced by any means, without the prior written permission of Stormbird Press, except in the case of brief quotations embodied in critical articles and reviews.

Cover design and typeset by Alice Teasdale, Big Quince Print, with Garamond Premier Pro.

National Library of Australia and State Library of South Australia Legal Deposit
Teasdale, Alice, 1974 – Author / Both, Júlia, 1993 – Illustrator

Letting the Summer Go
ISBN — 978-1-925856-58-3 (hbk)
ISBN — 978-1-925856-59-0 (pbk)

The publishing industry pulps millions of books every year when new titles fail to meet inflated sales projections—ploys designed to saturate the market, crowding out other books.

This unacceptable practice creates tragic levels of waste. Paper degrading in landfill releases methane—a greenhouse gas emission 23 times more potent than carbon dioxide.

Stormbird Press prints our books 'on demand', and from sustainable forestry sources, to conserve Earth's precious, finite resources.

We believe every printed book should find a home.

Letting the Summer Go

Alice Teasdale

Illustrated by Júlia Both

Today, we went back to our hidden garden.
We live in a new place now,
   so the garden has been left on its own all winter.
      And now it's spring, and it's a riot of wild!

An intrepid tangle of vegetables
and flowers towering
and cupping the shiny sky.

Last summer,
all the colour was stolen.

Everything left behind was jagged black,
>   leaking grey into the hazy, frightened air.
Even the light was bruised and grimy on my skin.
The only bright was the flash and whoop of red and blue.

"We need green!" said Mum.
So we went to our hidden garden
and pulled and piled and hosed and swept –

with the last hen, Ember, making sure we did it right.

But even the earth was shy and quiet, and smelled of dust and grey.
Nothing stirred or scuttled as Ember tapped and raked the empty dirt.

But then she made an excellent suggestion...

"Poo!" said Mum. "We need manure!"
So we shovelled and dug and tumbled and turned the soil back to life.

Our friends had bandaged us up with kindness
with clothes and food and toys
and, because they knew us well –

seeds, seeds, seeds
and tiny little plants!

So we went to the hidden garden
and scraped and scattered and pressed and patted
in rows and patches and pots and plots.

Ember was shut outside. "She'll peck it all up again!" said Mum.

Ember was not happy at all,
and because she couldn't have
all the tasty, tasty seeds
she tried to take my toe instead!
"She thinks you're a ladybird," said Mum.

"I am," I said.

Soon, the green shoots came,
shouldering aside crumbs of earth
and spreading open arms to the sun.

Some were almost too tiny to see.
Some fluttered like flags
and some poked out their tongues
to lick up the light.

One day it rained and rained!
Mum said we couldn't go to the garden
with all this rattling and roaring,
so I made my very own raincoat out of a bag,
and we went.

I watched the clouds in the puddles
and drew Ember's portrait out of mud.

The corn speared up and herbs spilled out,
the beans curled round

and pumpkin opened great umbrella leaves.

One day, the wind nagged and gusted and heaved and Ember was nowhere to be seen!

We went to the hidden garden, and discovered that the gale had niggled and jiggled at the gate
— and guess who we found inside?

She'd scritched and scratched
and tasted and torn
pecked and plucked and plundered

and done a poo in exactly the wrong spot!

We helped the garden mend itself,
 and when summer crept into autumn
 it was a feast and a forest,
 both at once!

Beans twined and tangled and dangled
pumpkins bulged and brightened
and the sweet-corn had so many ears
I asked what it wanted to hear.

There was enough for us, and all our friends –

and even enough for Ember!

"Now we can let the summer go," said Mum,
    and we were glad.

www.ingramcontent.com/pod-product-compliance
Lightning Source LLC
LaVergne TN
LVHW070908080426
835510LV00004B/123